BEDTIME,
EVERYBODY!
MORDICAI GERSTEIN

HYPERION BOOKS FOR CHILDREN / NEW YORK

This book is especially for Hugh Joseph Gerstein,
his big sister Daisy, and their aunt Risa.
Happy Bedtimes!
—M.G.

Printed in Singapore.
First Edition
1 3 5 7 9 10 8 6 4 2
The artwork for each picture is prepared using pen-and-ink and oil paint.
This book is set in 17-point VAG Rounded Light.
Designed by Joann Hill Lovinski.

Library of Congress Cataloging-in-Publication Data

Gerstein, Mordicai Bedtime, everybody! / Mordicai Gerstein — 1st ed.
p.   cm.
Summary: It is time for bed, but Daisy has a hard time getting her stuffed animals
to settle down.
ISBN 0-7868-0166-2 (trade) — ISBN 0-7868-2138-8 (lib. bdg.)
[1. Bedtime—Fiction. 2. Toys—Fiction.] I. Title
PZ7.G325Be   1996
[E]—dc20   95-36436

"Bedtime, everybody!" said Daisy.

"Not yet," said Bunny. "I haven't finished planting."
"Planting what?" asked Daisy.

"Carrots," answered Bunny. "Under the covers."
"I'm planting sunflowers," said Mouse.

"I'm diving for goldfish," said Duck.
"It's bedtime," said Daisy.

"I'm hungry," said Bear.

"I'm starving," said Pig.

"Let's eat," said Mouse.
"Let's have a picnic!" said Bunny.
"It's bedtime!" said Daisy.

"A BEDTIME PICNIC!" said everybody.
"With spaghetti and birthday cake," said Bunny.
"With ice cream and fried eggs," said Mouse.

"With hot dogs and jelly doughnuts and blueberry pancakes and coconut custard pie," said Bear.
"Pass the pickles," said Pig.

"It's bedtime," said Daisy.
"I have to brush my teeth," said Pig.

"You're stuffed," said Daisy. "You have no teeth."

"I want to brush them anyway," said Pig.
"Me too," said Duck.
"Me too," said Bunny.

"Me too," said Bear.
"Me too," said Mouse.
"Okay," said Daisy. "Now it's bedtime."

"I'm thirsty," said Bunny, "for orange juice."

"Grape juice," said Mouse.

"Milk," said Bear.

"Chocolate milk," said Pig.

"Hot chocolate," said Duck.

"It's very late," said Daisy.

"Mouse is poking me," said Bear.
"I am not," said Mouse. "Duck is kicking me."
"I am not!" said Duck. "Bear is tickling me."

"I am not!" said Bear. "I'm just scratching my nose."
"That's *my* nose," said Pig.
"Go to sleep," said Daisy.

"Mouse must tell a story," said Bear.
"Yes!" said everybody. "A story from Mouse."
"Where is Mouse?" asked Daisy.

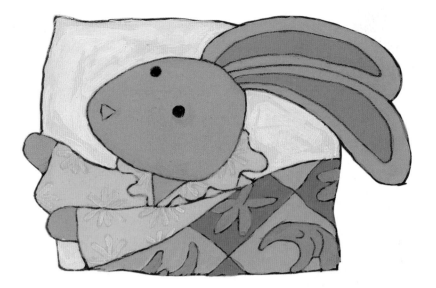

"Maybe she's under the covers," said Bunny. "I'll look."

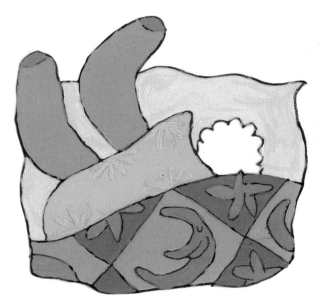

"She's not there!"

"MOUSE! WHERE ARE YOU?" called everybody.

"I fell under the bed,
    said Mouse.
"Tell us a story,"
    said Duck.
"Only if you rescue
    me," said Mouse.

"Under the bed is too far,"
      said Bunny.
"It's too dark,"
      said Duck.
"It's too scary," said Pig.
"I'll rescue you,
      Mouse," said Bear,
      "just as soon
      as I grow up."

"I will rescue Mouse," said Daisy.
"HOORAY!" said everybody.

"I'm back," said Mouse.
"A story, a story," cried everybody.

"Once upon a time," Mouse began,
    "there was a mouse . . ."
". . . and a bear," said Bear.
". . . and a pig," said Pig.

". . . and a bunny," said Bunny.
". . . and a hippopotamus," said Duck.
"And they all," said Mouse,
    "lived happily ever after."
"What about Daisy?" asked Pig.

"Shhhhh," whispered Bunny. "Daisy is sleeping."
"Good night," whispered Mouse.

"Good night, Mouse," whispered Bear, Bunny, and Pig.
"Is it morning yet?" asked Duck.

"It's bedtime," whispered everybody.
"Good night," whispered Duck.